WELCOME Beast Quest

Collect the special coins in this book.
You will earn one gold coin for
every chapter you read.

Once you have finished all the chapters,
find out what to do with your gold coins at
the back of the book.

With special thanks to Tabitha Jones

For Leo Loveridge

www.beast-quest.com

ORCHARD BOOKS

First published in Great Britain in 2017 by The Watts Publishing Group

1 3 5 7 9 10 8 6 4 2

Text © 2017 Beast Quest Limited.
Cover and inside illustrations by Steve Sims
© Beast Quest Limited 2017

Beast Quest is a registered trademark of Beast Quest Limited
Series created by Beast Quest Limited, London

A CIP catalogue record for this book is available from the British Library.

ISBN 978 1 40834 319 7

Printed in Great Britain

Orchard Books
An imprint of Hachette Children's Group
Part of The Watts Publishing Group Limited
Carmelite House, 50 Victoria Embankment, London EC4Y 0DZ

An Hachette UK Company
www.hachette.co.uk
www.hachettechildrens.co.uk

ZULOK
THE WINGED SPIRIT

BY ADAM BLADE

ORCHARD

CONTENTS

They thought I was dead, but death is not always the end.

My body was consumed in Ferno's dragon-fire, though that pain is a distant memory now. I have been trapped in this place – this Isle of Ghosts – for too long. It is time for me to remind my old enemies of my power.

The boundary between the realm of spirits and the realm of the living is like a thick castle wall – unbreakable by force or magic. But every castle has its weakness – someone on the inside who can lower the drawbridge. And I have found him. A weak wizard, but strong enough to do my bidding.

Hear me, Berric! Heed my summons. Open the way for me to return, and I will show Avantia that Evil like mine is impossible to kill.

Malvel

NOISES IN THE NIGHT

Tom jolted upright in bed, his heart pounding against his ribcage as he stared into the darkness. Black shapes lurked in the shadows, hunched like crouching Beasts. As Tom's eyes adjusted, the menacing forms became nothing but a chair draped with clothes, his nightstand, the brass fireguard. His pulse began to slow.

But what woke me?

Tom shivered and reached for the sweaty blankets tangled about his legs – then froze. A piercing cry filled the night. He leapt from his bed. *Someone's in trouble!* Tom grabbed his sword and dashed from the room. Then he heard the cry again, from somewhere above.

Cold flagstones sped beneath Tom's feet as he followed the corridor. The sound led him up a staircase, down a narrow passage then up more spiral stairs until he reached the door to the palace battlements. The terrible cry seemed

to come from just outside. Tom
thrust the door open, ready to fight.
Instead, soft grey silence greeted
him. The cry had stopped and dense
fog hid the palace rooftops.

"Who's there?" Tom called. No one
answered. As Tom stepped out, the
fog wrapped around him, muffling
his senses. The sharp tang of ice
crystals hung in the air, nipping
his nose. At first, Tom couldn't see
more than an arm's length ahead,
but then the fog swirled, revealing
the ghostly shadows of battlements
and towers. Something moved in
the greyness – a tall, dark form.
Tom tensed. It looked like a cloaked
and hooded man, striding along the

parapet wall. Tom's heart clenched
with alarm. Nothing separated the
strange figure from a deadly drop on
to cold, hard stone far below.

"Are you all right?" Tom called, his
voice ringing strangely in the cold

air. "You should be careful up there."

The figure didn't answer, but walked steadily away from him into the mist. Something about the figure's broad, straight shoulders caught at Tom's memory.

One of the king's men? But it seemed unlikely that Captain Harkman would post a watch with the king and queen away in Tangala. *An intruder, then?* Tom crept silently along the ramparts after the shadowy figure. His breath rose in white puffs before his face, mingling with the fog, and his bare feet soon turned numb with the cold. Once the figure reached the southern tower, it stopped and turned as if to gaze out over the hidden city.

"Hello!" Tom called. "Do you need help?"

The figure didn't move. Tom leapt softly on to the rampart wall and crept closer. The air around him seemed to grow colder still, tingling in his chest and making his muscles knot and quiver.

"Easy there," Tom said, keeping his voice as calm and steady as he could. "Why don't we just step back down?" He drew so close to the hooded form, he could almost reach out and touch it – but something held him back.

"Tom!" a deep, commanding voice said.

A fierce pang of emotion made Tom gasp and almost stagger. *Father!* The figure turned. Taladon's dark, piercing eyes looking back at him through the fog. Tom froze, his vision blurring with tears.

"Make haste to the Knight's Knoll,"

Taladon said, in a low, gravelly voice filled with urgency. "Do not delay!"

"Father, is it really you?" Tom asked, longing to believe his senses.

"The Knight's Knoll, Tom," Taladon repeated. "You must not fail – Avantia depends on you." Tendrils of mist swirled around Taladon's figure.

"Don't go!" Tom cried, his chest heaving with emotion, questions crowding his mind. "What's at the Knight's Knoll?"

"Hurry, Tom, before it's too late," Taladon's voice echoed hollowly.

A wave of grief crashed over Tom, making his throat ache and his eyes burn. He reached for his father, then his stomach gave a sickening lurch as his heel met no resistance and the solid brickwork dropped away...

"Tom!" Firm hands gripped his arm, steadying him, pulling him back.

It was Elenna, her brows pinched together with concern. "You almost fell off the roof!" she said.

"T-T-Taladon!" Tom stuttered through chattering teeth. His whole body shuddered with cold, though the strange chill had left the air. "Didn't you see him?"

Elenna's worried frown changed to a look of puzzled sorrow. "Oh, Tom," she said, "you must have been sleepwalking. It was just a dream. Come inside."

Tom shook his head. Raindrops began to patter against the rooftop, splattering his skin. In the distance, thunder rumbled. Tom's chest throbbed with a deep, hollow ache of longing for his father. "It wasn't a dream," Tom said. "Taladon sent me a warning from beyond the grave. Avantia's in danger."

"Are you sure?" Elenna asked, watching him closely.

Tom nodded. The mist flashed bluish-white briefly. A mighty clash of thunder sounded almost overhead.

"Then we must tell Daltec," Elenna said. She put a hand on Tom's soggy sleeve and steered him from the roof.

On the way to Daltec's chambers, Tom stopped by his own room and quickly scrambled into his tunic. By the time he and Elenna reached the wizard's tower, Tom's shivering had subsided, and he felt more like himself. Light spilled from beneath Daltec's door.

"Looks like he's still up," Elenna said.

Tom knocked. He opened the door to find Daltec at his desk. The usual spell books, herbs and potions had been pushed back, clearing a space for a weighty leather-bound tome filled with columns of numbers. Tom recognised it as the palace inventory. While the king and queen were in Tangala, Daltec had to keep the kingdom running.

The young wizard unbent from his work and peered at Tom and Elenna. "I would normally welcome an interruption from bookkeeping

at any time," he said, "but I sense you
two bring troubling news." Daltec
motioned Tom and Elenna towards
the fire. Tom took a seat, feeling his
muscles unlock as the heat crept
gradually over him.

Rain pelted the window, and the chamber lit up again and again with flashes of lightning as Tom recounted his tale. Thunder boomed and rumbled. Once Tom had finished, Daltec stood and paced the room.

"I can't pretend I know what this means," he said, "but..." Daltec stopped, his body suddenly tense as a flare of light filled the sky. He crossed to the window and gazed out. Thunder shook the tower. Once the sound had faded, Daltec beckoned Tom and Elenna to his side. "Come and look," he said, his voice heavy with dread.

Tom and Elenna joined Daltec at the sill. The fog had all but cleared. Another bolt of lightning crackled across the sky, striking towards the ground in a bright arc, like the lash of a whip. Tom gasped. The lightning was curved and snakelike, very different from the zigzagged forks he was used to.

"I have read about such lightning," Daltec said, "but had hoped never to see it. It is called Spirit Fire. It is said to mean the restless dead have been disturbed."

An icy chill washed over Tom. At his side, Elenna shivered. "That doesn't sound good," she said.

"No," Daltec said. "I believe it means a rift has been created between our world and the Isle of Ghosts."

THE KNIGHT'S KNOLL

"Why have I never heard of the Isle of Ghosts?" Tom asked, staring out at the storm. As he watched the strange lightning whip across the sky, his father's words echoed in his mind. Was Taladon's warning something to do with this rift? It had to be.

"It is rarely mentioned," Daltec

answered, "even within the Circle of Wizards. It is a dark and dangerous place, filled with evil far more terrifying than any fireside tale could conjure. If someone has disturbed the spirits on the isle, they are foolish indeed. It is said the ghosts of Evil Beasts are sent to dwell there for eternity."

Tom shuddered. "So if I go there I might face Beasts that I've defeated before – Evil Beasts, out for revenge?"

Daltec turned to gape at him, open-mouthed. "Go there? Never! The Isle of Ghosts is no place for mortals."

Tom shook his head. "I have

no choice. My father sent a clear warning. Avantia is in danger. If Evil ghosts have been disturbed, it is my duty to make sure they never find a way here."

"But you don't even know who is behind this," Daltec said.

"I do know *where* they are." Tom pointed into the distance where the lighting strikes converged, making the sky blaze with light. Each bright arc seemed to strike towards the same point on the landscape – the top of a steep, flat-topped hill said to be the tomb of Karlin the Great, a warrior of the past. The hill was known as Karlin's Barrow – but also by another, more ominous name.

"The Knight's Knoll," Tom said. "Daltec, can you magic me there?"

Daltec turned away. "Perhaps, but I won't. It's too dangerous."

"Please!" said Tom.

Daltec shook his head firmly. "Tom, Aduro would agree with me. You cannot go to the Isle of Ghosts."

"Fine," said Tom. He made for the door.

"Where are you going?" asked Daltec.

"I'm going to saddle Storm."

"And I'm coming too," said Elenna.

Leaving Daltec spluttering over his books, they ran to the stables.

Every second that passed seemed a second wasted. Whoever was causing the storm was at the Knight's Knoll already. He or she might even have opened a channel to the Isle of Ghosts.

Tom and Elenna worked quickly and silently to harness Storm, and soon they were galloping out of the castle gates. A fierce gust whirled about them, snatching at their clothes.

Tom kept his eyes on the sizzling blaze of energy ahead and squeezed Storm's flanks with his knees. Farmland, scrubland, rivers and trees flashed past. Curved bolts of lightning lashed over him and thunder rang in his ears.

Storm's mouth foamed as they charged over the fields. Taladon's voice replayed in Tom's mind. *Go*

now, before it's too late. Time passed,
but all Tom focused on was staying
in the saddle. His legs shook with the
effort. *Daltec might be right, but I
couldn't just sit in the palace. I had to
do something.*

There was no way of knowing how
long it had been, but gradually the
Knight's Knoll rose ahead of him. A
few hundred paces distant, Storm
stumbled and almost threw them. The
brave stallion was nearing collapse
– to ride him any further would be
cruel. Tom threw himself from the
saddle.

"I'll go on foot," he told Elenna,
and set off, using the speed of the leg
armour to fly across the landscape

many times faster than a normal
person could, towards the huge flat-
topped mound bathed in crackling
light. The night sky flickered and

flashed, filled with snaking bolts of energy, all lashing towards a glowing oval portal at the hill's summit. Tom squinted into the glare, and spotted the silhouette of a familiar bony figure standing before the blazing portal, arms raised and pale face lifted to the sky. Tom's jaw clenched. *Berric! He's behind this!*

LOST OPPORTUNITY

Anger and disgust surged through Tom. His fists clenched as he ran over the boggy ground, mud sucking at his boots and spattering his legs. *Whatever Berric's up to, I have to stop him!* Tom kicked harder, charging up the steep knoll, his hands and feet slipping again and again on the muddy slope. Finally, he reached the summit and stepped up on to level ground.

Berric stood with his back to Tom, staring up at the blinding display above. As Tom leapt forward, Berric turned. The young wizard's face twisted into a spiteful sneer. He lifted a hand and sent a bolt of energy fizzing towards Tom, who threw up his shield. *Crack!*

The shield bucked in his hands as if kicked by a horse, throwing him backwards into the mud. He scrambled to his feet, but already more blue light crackled between the wizard's palms. A triumphant spark shone in Berric's eyes as his thin lips spread into a smirk.

"You are too late to stop the magic I have unleashed," Berric cried, his voice cracking as he strained to be heard over the storm. "The next time you see me, I shall command an army of Beasts from the Isle of Ghosts. Avantia will be mine!"

Tom shook his head in rage and disbelief. "Berric!" he cried. "Don't do this! The Beasts you unleash will destroy you and everything else!"

"You underestimate my power!" Berric spat, then hurled the energy in his hands towards Tom.

Tom planted his feet wide and lifted his shield. *BOOM!* His arms buckled with the shock of the blow. Tom was thrown back, his

side hitting a rock and his shield tumbling from his grip and skidding down the hill. He staggered up, gasping for breath, clutching his throbbing ribs.

"Stop!" he cried. "You're making a terrible mistake!"

But Berric drew back his arms and hurled more magical energy his way. Tom leapt aside, and the bolt hit the grass, sending up clods of mud.

"You're the one making the mistake," Berric shouted, "by getting in my way!"

Tom lunged, but too late. Berric's next blast slammed into his shoulder, knocking him over the lip of the hill.

Tom hit the wet slope and tumbled down the bank. Light and darkness spun in his vision. Somehow he managed to grab a tuft of grass, jerking himself to a stop. He shook his head to clear the dizziness, then looked up to find Berric smiling down at him from the summit of the hill, surrounded by the pure white light of the portal. More sizzling energy crackled between Berric's palms. He turned them towards Tom.

"Goodbye, Master of the Beasts!" Berric cried.

Suddenly an arrow whizzed through the air, grazing Berric's

cheek. The young wizard ducked sideways, eyes wide with fear. Another arrow slashed through the fabric of his cloak. Berric dropped low to the ground, scanning the darkness with a furious scowl.

Tom craned his neck to see down the hill. *Storm!* Tom's stallion galloped across the plane, his hooves sending up sprays of mud and his black mane rippling in the wind. Elenna sat tall on the horse's saddle, fitting another arrow to her bow.

Berric gnashed his teeth with fury, then leapt to his feet and lunged towards the portal behind him.

Tom scrambled up, but he knew he'd never catch Berric now. He

spotted his shield nearby. Gripping
the edge, he flexed his wrist and
threw the disc of wood with all his
might. The shield spun through the
air. *This has to work!* But before
the shield could strike him, Berric

vanished through the portal.

All at once, everything went dark. Tom blinked to adjust his vision. Rain still lashed the hillside. The wind howled in his ears. But the rumble of thunder had fallen silent and the bright portal had vanished, leaving nothing but windswept grass.

I've failed!

Tom staggered to the top of the hill. His shield lay half buried in a puddle of mud. As Tom bent to retrieve it, he heard the splash of footsteps behind him. He turned to see Elenna hurrying towards him through the rain. And another shape appeared.

"Daltec! You came!"

The wizard nodded grimly. "I couldn't let you face this threat alone." He scanned the dark plateau. "So that's the end of Berric, then," he said. "I had hoped he would turn away from Evil, but it seems he has lost that chance."

"Berric said he would be back," Tom said. "He plans to bring Ghost Beasts to Avantia to take over the kingdom."

Daltec shook his head. "That's impossible. Now the portal is closed, there is no way back."

Tom stared at the muddy, sodden ground where the portal had been, then up at the dark and tattered sky. A memory of his father's troubled face on the battlements flashed through his mind. "I wish I could be so sure," he said. "My heart tells me this Quest isn't over. The kingdom is in danger. I can feel it."

The first grey rays of dawn slanted through the window of Aduro's tower, deepening the shadows on the former wizard's lined face as Tom finished his tale. Daltec and Elenna sat beside the embers of a dying fire, while Tom paced the room restlessly.

"So," Tom asked finally, "can Berric succeed? Is there any way to return from the Isle of Ghosts?"

Aduro fingered his beard for a

moment, his grey eyes narrowed in thought. Finally, he turned to Tom. "There is a way," he said. "I don't know it, and I do not think Berric is likely to find it. But, you asked me if it is possible. I believe it is. As everyone knows, the Knight's Knoll is named after Karlin – a great and powerful Master of Beasts. But what most people don't know is that Karlin went to the Isle of Ghosts. He returned so badly wounded that he died before he could tell anyone how he made it back. So you see, if even a Master of Beasts could not survive the passage, a young fool like Berric has little chance."

"As I told you, Tom," Daltec said,

"Berric's trapped on the Isle of Ghosts."

Tom paced on, his pulse quick and his mind racing. "No," he said. "If Karlin returned, that means Berric could open a way for Ghost Beasts to enter Avantia. I can't let that happen. I have to go after him."

Aduro shook his head. "If you do, you could become imprisoned for eternity in a realm of Evil. Leave Berric to that fate."

"But it is my duty to protect Avantia!" Tom said. "The risk of doing nothing is too great!"

"Tom," Aduro said sharply. "Think carefully before you act. If you choose to follow Berric to the Isle of

Ghosts, it will be the most dangerous
Quest you have faced, and with little
hope of success. You have a duty to
your kingdom, not to throw your life
away. Avantia needs its Master of
Beasts." Aduro's shoulders slumped,

and he suddenly looked older than ever. He covered his mouth and let out a stifled a yawn. "And this tired old man needs some sleep," he said. "We can discuss this further tomorrow, if we must."

Daltec, Tom and Elenna set off through the shadowy corridors of the palace towards their bedchambers. They walked in silence, eyes downcast, until Daltec took his leave. Then Elenna stopped. Tom turned towards her.

"We're going, aren't we?" Elenna asked.

Tom nodded. "Are you afraid?"

Elenna looked back at him steadily, almost fiercely. Then she let out a shaky laugh. "Petrified," she said. "I've never been so scared in my life. How about you?"

Tom grinned. "The same." His smile faded. "Whatever Aduro and Daltec say, I know deep down that the danger to Avantia is real. I keep thinking, *What would Taladon do?* And you know the answer to that as well as I do. Tomorrow we go to the Isle of Ghosts."

DALTEC'S PORTAL

Tom poked his egg with his fork, his stomach churning at the greasy smell. His eyes felt gritty with lack of sleep and his head ached, but he itched to be up and moving. On the bench beside him, Elenna sipped her tea. She hadn't even touched her porridge. At the head of the table Daltec ignored his bowl of porridge too, while Aduro, already finished, pushed back his chair. Once he'd gone, Tom put down his knife and fork.

"Daltec," he said. "Elenna and I need to talk with you."

Daltec froze, the spoon halfway to his mouth. He shook his head. "I know what you're going to ask."

"Aduro didn't forbid me from going," Tom cut in. "He said it was dangerous. That's not the same thing. The safety of Avantia is at stake. I have to go."

Daltec looked as unhappy as Tom had ever seen him, his brows pinched together as if searching for an argument. Tom felt a pang of guilt

– but there was no alternative. *I need
his help to protect the kingdom.*

"I suppose that is true," Daltec
said, at last. "But, Tom, are you really

sure you must do this? That there is no other way?"

Taladon's stern face flashed again through Tom's mind. "I've never been more certain," Tom said.

Daltec nodded. "Then I'll need some sort of token to create a conduit to the Isle of Ghosts – some connection with the dead," he said.

Tom thought for a moment. He had dealt with Ghost Beasts before – back when his father was still alive. He had freed Taladon from the Forbidden Land by repairing just such a token.

"Would the Amulet of Avantia do?" he asked.

Daltec pursed his lips thoughtfully.

"It might..." he said. "But—"

Tom got to his feet. "Then I'll fetch it. You and Elenna finish your breakfasts, then meet me on the battlements of the south tower."

Jumbled memories of the night filled Tom's mind as he made his way down shadowy passages and winding stairs towards the palace vaults. His father's warning, the strange scream, the unnatural lightning that had lashed the sky. He hurried on with his head down, letting his feet lead the way.

"Whoa!" Tom stopped with a jolt to see Aduro right before him. The old wizard had a huge pile of dusty books in his arms.

"Always a good idea to look where you're going!" Aduro said. "Where are you off to in such a hurry, anyway?"

Tom hesitated, his throat suddenly dry. "To the armoury," he said at last, giving as much of the truth as he could. "After seeing my father in that vision last night, I want to be with his possessions, like the Amulet of Avantia. It makes me feel nearer to him."

Aduro's frown softened to a sad smile.

"Taladon's death was a great loss to us all," he said. "I know he would be proud of you." The old wizard dipped his head in farewell and strode away along the corridor, his back bent with the weight of his books.

Tom face grew hot as he watched his old mentor go. He gritted his teeth and followed the passageway onward. *Aduro should understand how important this is!* But Tom still felt wretched inside.

A narrow staircase led him down to a torchlit stone passageway. Tom followed the dim tunnel and stopped at a heavy-looking door, padded with brass-studded leather. He took a small gold key from his pocket, unlocked the door and stepped inside. His Golden Armour stood in the centre of the small room, shining in the magical torchlight that blazed here in memory of his father. Behind the armour, a domed wooden trunk decorated with black ironwork stood against the wall. Tom bent and opened the trunk. The smell of oiled leather wafted out, mixed with wood smoke and other, fainter scents so tinged with memory Tom felt a choking lump in his throat. Taladon's possessions rested neatly side by side – belts, tunics, a bone-handled knife, a silver drinking cup. Tom lifted a small object wrapped in velvet. He unfolded the cloth, letting the cold, heavy talisman slide out into his hand. The silver-and-blue amulet shone as brightly as the day Tom had used

it to free his father from Malvel's evil. Tom tucked it into his tunic pocket and hurried away.

Bright sunlight glinted off wet stone, making Tom blink as he stepped out on to the roof. Daltec and Elenna stood at the parapet looking out over the city. Tom crossed to their side. The whole of Avantia looked washed clean and fresh. Slate rooftops shone like silver; red and gold flags flapped in the breeze and white clouds scudded across the sky over fields of emerald green. Elenna and Daltec turned. In the bright morning light, their tired, worried faces looked almost grey.

"Do you have the amulet?" Daltec asked.

Tom nodded, handing the blue-and-silver disc to the wizard. Daltec studied it for a long moment, chewing his lip. When Daltec finally lifted his eyes to Tom, he looked anxious and very young – more like the apprentice Tom had once known than the powerful wizard Daltec had become.

"The island exists on a different plane of reality from our world," Daltec said. "If this goes wrong, I don't know where you'll end up."

Elenna put a hand on Daltec's sleeve. "We trust you," she said.

Tom forced a chuckle. "From what you've told us, anywhere would be safer than the Isle of Ghosts, anyway."

He'd been trying to calm his friend, but if anything, Daltec looked paler than he had done before.

"You can do this," Tom said. Daltec nodded, then covered the amulet with his hand. He bowed his head and started to chant.

Almost at once, Tom heard a sighing moan of wind. The brightness of the morning faded, as if a cloud had hidden the sun, and Tom felt suddenly cold. Elenna rubbed her arms. A hideous buzzing started up, low at first, but growing louder until it seemed to fill Tom's head. He felt sick and dizzy. Dark specks swarmed in his vision. Tom shook his head and rubbed his eyes, but the spots remained. More appeared, humming around him like a cloud of flies. The black dots drew together in the air just beyond the battlements, gradually forming an irregular, shifting inky blot about the size of a door. The terrible noise came from the darkness, growing so loud Tom could hardly bear it. A rotting stench filled his nostrils, making him want to retch. He suddenly realised Daltec had fallen silent.

He turned to find his friend watching him. "No one has ever returned from the Isle of Ghosts and lived," Daltec said. "I will be praying that you two are the first. Now go, before the portal fades."

Tom shot Elenna what he hoped was an encouraging smile. She smiled

back, wide-eyed, tight-lipped, but resolved. They exchanged a nod, then leapt over the battlements into stinking, buzzing blackness.

THE WINGED SPIRIT

Tom felt as though he'd leapt into treacle, or become trapped in thick tree sap like an insect. He wasn't falling, but he couldn't move his limbs. The buzzing in his ears grew wild and shrill. Suddenly, what felt like hundreds of flies rushed at him, battering against his skin, filling his nose and fluttering against his lips, trying to get into his mouth. He couldn't breathe or see. Panic rose in his chest. Then, all at once, the fluttering stopped; everything grew silent.

Tom opened his eyes. At first he could see nothing but a deep, brownish gloom filled with shadows. But as his vision adjusted to the dimness he found he was standing in a barren wasteland of dusty boulders and rocky peaks beneath a sunless sky the colour of dried blood.

"The Isle of Ghosts..." Elenna breathed beside him.

When he glanced her way, his stomach lurched. Her eyes were

sunken deep into her skull, and were
black, with no iris or white. Her skin
looked sallow, and stretched too thin
over hollow, bony cheeks.

"Are you all right?" Elenna asked.
The strange vision was gone. She
was herself again.

Tom nodded, but his mouth felt as dry as dust. What had he just seen? A magical effect of being in the Isle of Ghosts? Or some kind of glimpse into the future? "I thought you... Don't worry."

"Which way, then?" Elenna asked, peering doubtfully into the gloom. Then she pointed. "Look!"

Tom followed the line of her finger. Beyond rock pillars and boulders, he could just make out a broad, cloaked form trudging over a mound of loose scree towards the foot of a craggy hill.

"Does it look...familiar to you?" Elenna asked.

Tom nodded. Something about

the way the figure moved, straight-backed with long steady strides, did look familiar. It reminded Tom of the figure on the roof. He called on the power of his golden helmet for a better view, but the harder he looked, the deeper the shadowy gloom became. It seemed to press in on him, a thick, malevolent substance, blocking his sight. *Perhaps my Golden Armour doesn't help me here...*

"I think it could be my father," Tom said, hearing a catch of emotion in his own voice. "But I'm not sure."

"Then we'd better be careful," Elenna said.

Tom nodded. A part of him longed

to dash headlong towards his father. But he knew Elenna was right. It could be a trick. "Let's follow," Tom said.

He soon realised that was far easier said than done. Their boots crunched on loose shingle, sinking deep with every step. Larger boulders twisted or rolled away from under their feet. What looked like steady platforms of rock toppled suddenly, making them stumble. Other rocks crumbled to dust beneath their boots – dust that seemed to move, wriggling away into cracks.

The figure ahead walked slowly but easily up the scree, while Tom and Elenna slipped and scrambled, tripped and fell. By the time they reached the base of the crag, Tom's shins throbbed with bruises and Elenna was limping, her lips pressed together with pain. He looked up to see the hooded man round a bend in the rock, dipping out of sight. Tom clambered after him, but when he and Elenna turned the corner, they found no sign of the figure.

"Great!" Elenna said. "Now what?"

Tom looked about. Huge layers of rock rose above them, piled on top of each other like giant steps. At the top of the crag, broken fingers of stone, like misshapen spires, jutted into the sunless sky.

"If we keep going, maybe we'll find him," Tom said.

They clambered on up the rock face, scrambling at first, but soon climbing hand over hand, until Tom's arm muscles burned and his fingers ached. When Tom glanced back, he found the barren landscape hidden beneath a thick blanket of shadow. Above, the dark red sky hung like a heavy shroud with no moon or stars to light the way. Together, Tom and Elenna pulled themselves up on to a shelf of rock. Tom stood panting, staring in awe at what he and Elenna had found. A huge, scrappy pile of dead, leafless branches, spattered with globs of grey and white, and intertwined with what looked like bones, had been built up against the rocky wall. The pungent stink of rotten fish caught in Tom's throat and made his eyes sting. Poking from the top of the pile of bones and twigs rose a smooth white dome, speckled brown and gold – an egg big enough to hold a fully grown vulture.

"It's a nest," Elenna said. "But it's huge. And what kind of animal could survive in a place like this?"

"Not an animal," Tom said. "A Beast." He felt a trembling in his chest, and heard a brittle pattering from above, then a rumbling sound.

"Avalanche!" he cried, pulling Elenna aside just as a boulder thundered past. More followed, bouncing and crashing down the rock face.

Tom and Elenna scrambled back over the cliff edge to rest on footholds. Tom pressed himself tight to the rock as boulders tumbled all around them. Finally, the clattering of rocks stopped.

"I think it's clear," Tom said. He climbed up and peered over the lip of the cliff. On another shelf of rock not far above them, a slender figure stood, his hands lifted above his head and a spiteful grin plastered across his face. "It's Berric!" Tom hissed. "He must have caused the avalanche."

Berric let his arms fall, then clambered down the rock face to stand beside the giant nest. He reached inside and lifted out the speckled egg, cradling it in his arms.

Tom could hardly believe what he was seeing. Anger swelled inside him. *He's stealing the Beast's egg!* Tom vaulted up on to the plateau, closely followed by Elenna.

"Berric! Stop!"

Berric lifted his eyes to Tom. "Oh, you survived?" the wizard said. "Never mind. You're too late to stop me." He hugged the vast egg to his chest, his pale eyes glinting in the low light.

"We won't have to!" Elenna said. "That egg belongs to a Beast. It's not going to let you just take it!"

"That's what I'm counting on," Berric said, smiling. Tom heard the sweep of wings from above them. Berric's smile broadened into a crazed grin at the sound. "You're about to meet Zulok," he cried.

Keeaaaah! A shrill cry rent the air.

Tom looked up to see two blazing orbs of light streaking towards them through the gloomy sky, casting long white beams. The beams swept downwards, and Tom squinted, shading his eyes from the piercing brightness that flooded the plateau.

As the lights drew closer, Tom made out broad dark wings behind them, and a fanned tail. With a shock of alarm, he recognised the shining orbs for what they were – the eyes of a giant eagle. The twin beams locked on Berric, turning his white hair and pale skin silver, but Berric grinned like a child with a prize. The bird angled downwards, threw back its wings and dived, bathing the

skinny wizard in searing light, as he clutched the giant egg.

"What's he up to?" Tom said.

"Surely he's not trying to get himself killed?"

Tom and Elenna ducked as the Beast swept over their heads, cruel, pincer-like claws outstretched. Berric set the egg down, then drew back his arms and made a gesture as if flinging something. A vast red glowing net unfurled before him, straight into the eagle's path. The Beast flapped its wings frantically, trying to slow its descent, but it was too late. It slammed into the net. Red twines closed about, tangling around its wings and pinning them to its body. Berric stepped neatly aside as the eagle ploughed breast-first into the stone ledge and tumbled over, its claws and feathers entwined in the net. Berric leapt towards the trapped eagle, and tugged a dagger from his belt.

"Now I shall slay this Beast," Berric cried. "Then I will have earned a key to open a portal back to Avantia." He turned to Tom, eyes flashing.

What does he mean by a 'key'?

"All the Beasts from this land will flood through. Avantia will be mine!" Berric's knife flashed downwards.

1

6

RAGE OF THE BEAST

"No!" Tom leapt forwards, sword in hand. At the same moment, the Beast bucked inside the net. One mighty wing sprang free of the cords, swiping Berric's legs out from under him. Berric landed hard on his back, his knife skittering away across the rock. Zulok thrashed

and squawked, a furious bundle
of feathers and claws, crisscrossed
with glowing red strands. Berric
tried to scramble away, his eyes
wide with terror, but the panicked
bird rolled over his legs. The netting
snagged Berric's ankles, pulling him
along as the bird flapped, trying to
get free.

"Help!" Berric shouted,
desperately squirming to dodge the
Beast's sharp talons and snapping
beak.

Tom realised they were about to
tumble off the plateau. He gritted
his teeth. *Berric might be an evil
fool, but I can't let him die...*

Tom lunged forwards, making a

grab for the net, but the panicked flailing of the bird wrenched the cord from his fingers. The trapped eagle tumbled over the cliff edge, dragging Berric with her.

The evil sorcerer screamed. Tom threw himself into a dive, snatching for Berric's arm just as the wizard slid off the cliff. His fingers closed about Berric's wrist and the full weight of the boy and the Beast yanked his arm downwards. Tom braced his body against the rocky ledge and called on the power of his Golden Armour. His arms shook and every muscle in his body strained, but it was no good. He wasn't strong enough to lift them.

"Elenna! Help!" Tom cried from between clenched teeth.

Elenna already had an arrow in her bow. She leaned over the ledge and aimed at the netting tangled about

Berric's legs, then let fly. The arrow slashed through a cord, freeing one leg. Another arrow followed the first, severing more twines. With the third arrow, Berric flew free. Tom tumbled backwards, dragging Berric with him on to the plateau. Zulok plummeted down the cliff face.

Berric scrambled away from Tom, then stood rubbing at a graze on his elbow, scowling furiously. Glowing red netting trailed on the ground at his feet, still draped around one ankle. "I hope that stupid bird falls to her death!" Berric spat.

"You're not going to thank us for saving your life, then?" Elenna said.

Berric glowered back at her as he unhooked the red net from his feet. Tom drew his sword and stepped towards him.

"You're in my custody now," Tom said. But as he spoke, silver light flooded the plateau and a shriek of rage filled the air. Tom turned to see Zulok flapping towards them, her giant claws reaching for Berric and her huge eyes shining like twin suns. Berric snatched the remainder of his red net from the ground and lashed it at the bird.

"Get away from me!" he screeched. The giant eagle squawked and wheeled away, but then swooped in again for another swipe.

"Don't just stand there! Kill it,"
Berric shouted at Tom. "Isn't that
what a Master of Beasts is for?"
Berric lashed at Zulok again with
his net.

The Beast flapped hard, turning
suddenly to dodge the magical
rope. The edge of one massive wing
clipped Berric across the temple.
The boy dropped like a sack of
grain, knocked out cold.

Zulok wheeled around, circling in
the twilight, then came in to hover
before the plateau, watching Tom
and Elenna, her beacon-like eyes
filled with rage.

Tom squinted into the light, and
put a hand to the red jewel in his

belt. *We mean you no harm. We will
leave you and your egg in peace,*
he told the Beast, communicating
through the power of the jewel. He

bent slowly, one arm shielding his eyes, and lowered his sword to the ground.

"Tom, what are you doing?" Elenna asked.

"Quick! Find the egg!" Tom hissed back.

Zulok's vast wings beat the air. Her bright eyes narrowed, as if in thought. *She's listening!*

I am here to take the wizard who tried to steal your egg away from this realm, Tom told her. Zulok cocked her head as if considering, and Tom felt a glimmer of hope.

"Tom!" Elenna hissed from behind him.

Tom glanced back to see her

standing beside Zulok's nest, carefully placing the egg back inside. Heavy dread settled in Tom's gut. A long crack ran from a crumpled dent in the top of the egg, down the shell, almost to the base. It looked like a breakfast egg that had been hit by a spoon. *It's broken!*

Tom turned back to the Beast to see her glowing eyes widen in horror as they rested on her damaged egg, only to flicker and blaze brighter still.

The Beast opened her vast beak wide, and a furious screech filled Tom's senses, so loud he staggered and fell to his knees. Once the terrible cry faded, Tom blinked his aching eyes, and glanced up. Zulok hovered in the sunless sky before them, vast, majestic, furious and almost too painful to look at.

The piercing shriek of her voice filled Tom's mind. *You broke my egg! Now you shall all perish!*

BLIND KNIGHTS

Tom leapt to his feet as the furious eagle swept towards him. Peering into the searing light cast by Zulok's eyes, Tom could just make out the spread of her mighty wings and the curve of her talons slicing the air. He glanced back to see Elenna beside the nest, squinting along the length of an arrow. Her aim looked wildly off. *She can't see to shoot!*

Tom lifted his sword. But as he faced the Beast, white light flooded his own vision. Dazzled, he turned and ran. *Crunch!* Tom heard the eagle's claws slam into

the rock behind him. The bird let out a screech of rage. Tom ran on, the wind from Zulok's wingbeats pounding his body. The rear wall of the rocky shelf loomed before him – a dead end – but Tom sprinted harder. He leapt, running up the wall in two long strides, then kicked off, flipping himself backwards. He tucked his body as he spun, diving over Zulok's head. He landed on his feet to see the bird plough straight into the wall. She crumpled to the ground in a mass of dark feathers, then flexed her wings, shook herself and rose to her feet.

"Give me the key, you dumb animal!" a piping, nasal voice cried.

Berric!

The scrawny boy staggered past Tom, his eyes unfocused, but his face red with fury. He had found his knife, and held it drawn back, ready to strike the bird. Tom didn't understand. What was the 'key' he spoke of?

"Give it to me!" Berric screamed again. The Beast's vast head turned. Her white eyes flashed, focusing on the young wizard. Elenna leapt from the shadow of Zulok's nest and cannoned into Berric's knees, tackling him to the ground. Berric twisted in her grip, swiping with his knife, but Elenna caught his wrist and held it fast. Berric writhed and bucked, but Tom could see Elenna was stronger.

"I'll handle him!" she shouted to Tom.

He turned his attention to Zulok. The huge bird stood tall now, fully recovered from her fall. Tom grabbed the red jewel in his belt, hoping to reason with the Beast.

We are not here to harm you. We were trying to protect your egg from the wizard.

Zulok's eyes narrowed, burning with rage. She opened her cruel beak and let out a ragged caw of fury. *You broke my egg! Now you shall die!*

Tom felt the power of the Beast's

rage and knew the time for reason
had passed. Zulok reared up and
opened her vast, black wings. She
lifted her head high and puffed out
her breast. To Tom's amazement
and horror, the dark feathers there
parted to reveal a pair of huge,
lidded eyes. Zulok let out a terrific
cry of rage and the new eyes opened
wide, brighter than the sun. Tom
blinked and squinted against the
searing light, trying to peer into
the glare. But even opening his eyes
a tiny crack burned like scalding
blades plunging into his skull. *I'm
completely blind!*

Tom heard the swish of wingbeats
and backed away. His heel teetered

over the edge of the cliff, making his heart leap into his throat. He caught his balance, but had nowhere to go. *I'm trapped...* A gust of wind buffeted his face. *The Beast is attacking!* Tom dived to one side. *BOOF!* A huge weight slammed into his shoulder, sending him spinning. His back smashed against the rocky ground, blasting the air from his lungs. The shock made his eyes flicker open, but a stab of white-hot pain forced them shut again. He could hear the brittle clack of talons on rock close by. The light behind his eyelids blazed brighter as the Beast loomed over him. Something razor-sharp raked across his chest.

"Aargh!" Tom tried to scramble away, but more pain flared in his shoulder as the Beast struck again. Rough talons clamped down over his chest, making him gasp, pinning him to the ground. *Please, no!* He flinched, his muscles tight, expecting any moment to feel a deadly blow from the Beast's cruel beak. *This is the end... I've failed.*

His ears picked up the sound of bodies scuffling. *Elenna and Berric.* He needed to help his friend.

But then a feeling of peace washed over him – a steady, comforting calmness like the embrace of strong, loving arms.

"Father?" he croaked.

Taladon's voice spoke right by
Tom's ear, as clear as it had been
on the battlements – but it was
strangely distant, as if Taladon was
several horse-lengths away. "Blind
Knights, Tom," he said.

The words took Tom straight
back to his youth at the forge.
Blind Knights was a game Uncle
Henry had taught him. Henry and
Taladon had invented it as boys –
a blindfolded sparring session to

heighten the senses and train the
mind.

Maybe... Tom thought, grasping at
hope, *maybe I can fight this Beast*.
But then Zulok's talons tightened
over Tom's chest, squeezing the air
from his lungs and bringing his
terror rushing back with full force.

FIGHTING BLIND

Ignoring the pain in his chest from the Beast's mighty claws, Tom gritted his teeth and tightened his fist on his sword hilt. *Blind Knights, for you, Father*, he vowed. *While there's blood in my veins, I will try.*

Tom let his mind go blank, just like he had done when playing

Blind Knights as a child. He
stopped trying to see with his eyes,
and let his other senses grow sharp.

A soft sigh like the swish of a
scythe told him something was
coming. The faintest breeze stirred
the hairs on his cheek. He threw

up his shield. *Thud!* The Beast's beak slammed into the wood. Zulok hissed with rage. Tom lifted his arm and stabbed his sword down into the talons clamped around his chest. The Beast screeched and Tom felt the pressure lift. *I'm free!* He scrambled to his feet, using his red jewel to sense for the Beast. The force of Zulok's rage crashed over him like a wave. He could feel the pent-up fury flowing through her body – the fierce desire to slash and tear. The Beast's ferocious need to protect her young made him tremble with awe. Tom heard a faint whistle of wind. He lifted his sword, parrying the blow, then thrust it forward.

The blade met only air. Pain flared in his shoulder and he staggered back. *I can't do it!* But then a low voice spoke in his ear, warm and calm.

"Close…" Taladon said. "Keep focus, Master of the Beasts."

Sweat poured from Tom's tense body, making the grip on his sword slick. He drew a deep breath. *If my father has the power to reach me from beyond the grave, surely I can do this!* He swallowed hard, reaching out with his mind…

And this time he felt the Beast's movements almost as if they were his own. He knew without doubt

where her talons would land. He
swiped with his sword and felt a
dull thud as it hit. *Yes!*

Zulok hissed with fury. Tom felt
the air stir as if parted by a blade.
His sword arm flashed out, swiping
upwards. *Crack!* The blade smashed

across something hard – a talon or beak.

The Beast screeched. Tom sensed another attack coming. He called on the power of his golden breastplate and swung his shield with all his strength, knocking a fierce blow aside.

Before the Beast could come at him again, Tom lunged, slicing sideways with his sword. His blade slashed though feathers like a sickle through grass. Zulok squawked with rage. Tom pressed on, swiping and jabbing, severing more feathers,

his shield blocking blow after blow.
She's slowing down... Her anger still
burned but he could tell that her
body was getting tired. He called on
the power of his golden boots and
leapt, swiping his blade downwards.
The tip of his sword raked flesh.

Keeaaaah! Zulok cried. Tom felt
her fury turn to terror. The searing
light behind his eyes faded to the
red of his lids. Cautiously, Tom
opened his eyes. He found the
dim plateau of rock shrouded in
shadow. Zulok cowered against the
rock face beside her nest, one wing
folded, the other hanging limp.
The magical eyes in her chest had
vanished and her gaze had dimmed

to a silvery glow. Elenna crouched nearby, blinking to adjust her eyes. A bruise ran along her cheekbone, and there was no sign of Berric. Something moved in the shadows, half hidden by the Beast's scaled legs – something damp and pink, with tufts of feathers. *A chick!*

Tom thrust his sword into his belt, then took a step forwards. Zulok threw her good wing before her chick, and let out a hiss of alarm.

"I don't want to hurt you or your chick!" Tom told her. "I didn't come here to kill Beasts." Tom reached for Epos's healing talon in his shield. "I can heal your wing if you will let me." But as Tom approached, Zulok

drew back, gripping her chick with
one pincer-like foot. She spread her
wings and beat them hard, buffeting
Tom with wind. Her injured wing
looked slightly crooked, but it lifted
the Beast and her chick into the air.
With a flurry of mighty wingbeats,
Zulok powered into the red-brown
sky. Her eyes flared suddenly,
glowing bright as she hovered above
the plateau. Then the Beast swooped
away, quickly vanishing into the
gloom.

Tom sagged with exhausted relief.

"You did it!" Elenna said, stepping
to his side.

"We failed," said Tom. "I injured a
Good Beast."

Elenna pointed to the ground at Tom's feet. "But I think she left you something."

Tom peered down to find a small black feather, about the length of his hand. As he bent to retrieve it, he realised it was actually metal. And when he studied it more closely, he noticed its black barbs

looked almost like the notches of a key.

"Maybe this is the key Berric was after," Tom said, turning it over. "It must open a gateway back to our world."

Elenna nodded. "Unfortunately Berric managed to weasel out of my grip while we were all blind, so we can't ask him. He's probably slunk away to try his luck with a new Beast."

"We'll have to go after him," Tom said, turning to scan the barren landscape for any sign of the boy. He gasped with shock at what he saw, and leapt forwards. The cloaked figure they had followed to the crag stood right at the edge of the cliff, staring out over the rocky terrain.

"Father?" Tom cried, covering the ground with swift strides. He reached out to touch Taladon's shoulder. But instead of landing on cloth, his hand fell through empty air, so cold it burned his flesh.

Tom staggered back, clutching his hand to his chest. The figure before him turned slowly, then tossed back its hood. Elenna let out a short cry. Tom felt his body go numb. Instead of his father's stern, handsome features, Tom saw cruel, thin lips, spread into an evil smile, beneath a hooked nose and deep-set eyes the

colour of coal. The hooded figure
had not been Taladon – it was Tom's
oldest enemy. Malvel.

"Welcome to my world," the Dark
Wizard said, the hideous rasp of his

voice grating like a rusty saw. "Make yourself comfortable, won't you, for you shall never leave!"

The wizard tipped back his head and laughed, the sharp planes of his face fading into the gloom, until Tom realised he was staring at nothing. He turned back to Elenna, the ghostly echo of evil laugher still ringing in his ears. She, too, was staring wide-eyed at where Malvel had been. Elenna blinked and met his gaze. "Tom, how can this be possible?"

"I don't know," Tom gasped. "Not only is my father here, but Malvel is too…"

They had ignored Aduro's warning

and walked straight into their greatest enemy's trap. "Berric must have been working for Malvel all along," said Tom.

This Quest just became deadlier than ever.

THE END

CONGRATULATIONS, YOU HAVE COMPLETED THIS QUEST!

At the end of each chapter you were awarded a special gold coin.
The QUEST in this book was worth an amazing 8 coins.

Look at the Beast Quest totem picture inside the back cover of this book to see how far you've come in your journey to become

MASTER OF THE BEASTS.

The more books you read, the more coins you will collect!

Do you want your own
Beast Quest Totem?

1. Cut out and collect the coin below
2. Go to the Beast Quest website
3. Download and print out your totem
4. Add your coin to the totem
www.beastquest.co.uk/totem

Don't miss the next exciting Beast Quest book, SKALIX THE SNAPPING HORROR!

Read on for a sneak peek...

RIDER OF THE GHOST WOLF

Tom stared into the empty space where the Dark Wizard Malvel had been standing only a moment ago.

"It can't be..." he said, gasping. "It's not possible!"

The sneering figure of his old

enemy had vanished into thin air, but Malvel's parting words still rang in Tom's ears.

Welcome to my world... You shall never leave!

Elenna's eyes were wide with disbelief. "But Malvel is dead," she said. "Burned to ash by Ferno's fire."

"In this place, the dead have all the power," Tom replied grimly. "And if we don't defeat him here, he may find a way to return to Avantia." He gritted his teeth. "That must not happen."

The rocks rose up around them like shards of broken bone. The sky was full of racing clouds. The wind hissed and shrieked through the mountains.

The Isle of Ghosts truly was a terrible place. The Evil Wizard Berric had opened a portal, and planned to bring back an army of Beasts to Avantia. Their old friend Aduro had warned them to stay away, but how could Tom do that? His own father Taladon had come to him in a vision, urging him to help. The words were burned into Tom's brain.

You must not fail. Avantia depends on you!

And so they had come, using the Amulet of Avantia and the Wizard Daltec's ancient spell.

Tom gazed out over the edge of the high cliff where they stood. *Berric's still out there.* Tom and Elenna had

managed to stop the young wizard
from capturing Zulok, a giant bird
Beast. But Berric had escaped. Tom
reached his hand into his pocket
and took out the metal feather left
by Zulok. It was a key that would
open a portal back to Avantia. *But*

we can't leave Berric here – he'll find
another key eventually and return to
Avantia with his Beast army.

"Something's coming," murmured
Elenna, interrupting Tom's dark
thoughts. She was pointing into the
grey sky, where a shape was hurtling

towards them through the clouds.

Tom's hand moved to the hilt of his sword. "Another flying Beast?" His battle with Zulok had been gruelling, and he wasn't sure he had the strength to fight off another Beast so soon.

He called on the power of the golden helmet, and squinted into the sky.

What he saw chilled his blood.

It was a giant black wolf, soaring towards them on wide, leathery wings. Tom had never seen this Beast before...but something about it haunted his memory.

With an ashen face, Elenna slotted an arrow on to her bowstring.

As Tom watched the Beast dip its wings and rush closer, he drew his sword. The wolf's mouth opened, his fangs gleaming like knives.

Elenna closed an eye to aim. "I'll fire a warning shot," she said.

"Wait!" Tom struck the end of her bow with his hand.

Elenna gave him a startled look. "What is it?"

Tom focused on a dark shape behind the wolf's shaggy head. "There's a rider," he cried, "seated between the wings. Do you see?"

"I do," said Elenna, as the flying wolf swept lower.

The figure astride the Beast's wide back was wearing a hood that shadowed his face.

"Could it be Malvel coming back already?" asked Elenna.

"Not if he's got any sense," said Tom, his fingers tightening on his sword hilt.

The giant wolf thumped on to the rocky ground. His long black tongue lolled from his powerful jaws. Tom could smell the strong odour of the creature's matted fur.

Tom raised his sword. "Show yourself!" he called to the hooded figure.

The person drew back their hood, revealing a noble face with a golden beard and swept-back golden hair. Tom's heart leapt for joy.

"Father!" Sheathing his sword, Tom ran forward as his father climbed down from the Beast's back.

"You are sharp-eyed, my son!"

Taladon said, with a wide smile.

Tom reached out to hug his father, but stumbled right through him.

"I would embrace you if I could." Taladon sighed. "But it is impossible."

Tom felt a weight sink through his chest. He smiled ruefully. "I almost forgot you were…" His voice faltered.

"Dead?" said Taladon gently. "I am, my son. And so is Gulkien." Taladon patted the winged wolf.

Read
SKALIX THE SNAPPING HORROR
to find out what happens next!